Alice Savage

MONA

Alice Savage grew up in a theatrical family and began writing plays in the fifth grade. As an English teacher of adult learners, she combines creative writing with a deep awareness of language to illuminate the worlds of immigrants and cultural explorers. She credits her multi-cultural family as inspiration. An author on many course books for Oxford University Press, Cambridge University Press, Pearson, and others, Alice has presented widely on the role of drama in language learning. She has published several award-winning one-act plays. Her dramatic fiction shows happens when characters address challenges for which they may or may not be prepared. Alice lives in Houston.

First published by Gemma in 2024.

www.gemmamedia.org

Printed in the United States of America

978-1-956476-36-1

Library of Congress Cataloging-in Publication Data available.

Cover by Laura Shaw Design

Named after the brightest star in the Northern Crown, Gemma is a nonprofit organization that helps new readers acquire English language literacy skills with relevant, engaging books, eBooks, and audiobooks. Always original, never adapted, these stories introduce adults and young adults to the life-changing power of reading.

Open Door

To mothers around the world

TABLE OF CONTENTS

Morning sun comes through the trees. It shines into an upstairs bedroom window. Mona sits up in bed. Her heart is beating fast, and she looks around in fear. There are white flowers on a table. Her suitcase is on a chair. She is safe.

A photo of her husband is next to the bed. He is wearing a doctor's coat and standing outside the hospital in Aleppo, Syria. Mona picks up the photo and holds it to her heart. "I miss you," she says in Arabic.

Then Mona hears her son's laughter. Rashid is downstairs, and he sounds happy. Mona smiles. Rashid is safe, also.

Mona dresses quickly and goes down to breakfast. Rashid is at the table with

Mona's brother-in-law, Joe. Both of them are tall and thin with thick dark hair. Joe's American wife, Brita, is in the kitchen. Brita has green eyes and red hair. Brita is wearing exercise clothes and shoes in the house.

"Good morning," says Brita. She brings Mona a glass of tea. Mona tastes her tea. It is hot and bitter. She sets it down and waits for Brita to offer her sugar. Brita returns with a plate of flat bread, cheese, nuts, and fresh herbs. Brita learned about Syrian breakfasts from her husband Joe, but she forgets the sugar. Mona is still a guest, so she does not ask.

Rashid and Joe are talking about the bus. Rashid takes two buses every day. First, he goes to college. After class, he takes two buses back to the neighbor-hood. Then Rashid goes to work.

"I am on the bus for three hours," Rashid says.

"That's a long time!" Brita comes back. She puts pancakes on the table, and calls her two sons, Kyle, who is five, and Ethan, three, to come for breakfast.

Mona looks at the pancakes. They are not bread, and they are not cake.

"Go ahead," says Joe, "take one."

"No, thank you," she says politely.

"Okay, then I will!" says Rashid. He takes two pancakes. Then he sees his mother watching.

"Don't be afraid mom. They're not going to bite you!" Rashid eats his pan-cake. Then he takes another pancake.

"Yum," he says.

Mona watches Rashid eat.

The third time Rashid offers, Mona finally nods. He puts a pancake on her plate and pours honey on it. Mona takes a bite. It is sweet, and it tastes good with the strong tea.

"Yum," she says, and Rashid laughs.

Mona smiles at her son. *This is his new life*, she thinks. *And it is mine also.*

Joe has a small business on Nineteenth Street. He helps people mail things. Today he is working at home. When he hears voices, he leaves his computer and comes into the kitchen. Mona is with Brita and their son Kyle. They are looking at a big pile of coins on the kitchen table.

"That's a lot of money!" says Kyle.

"We're going to take these coins to the bank," says Brita. She shows him the paper rolls. There is one size for quarters and smaller ones for other coins. "We'll fill these rolls with coins, and then the bank will take them."

"Hey, Kyle," says Joe. "I have a math

question for you. How many quarters
are there in one dollar?"

Kyle looks at his father, "Everyone
knows that dad. Four!"

"Okay, so there are four quarters in
a dollar. Now here's my question: a roll
has forty quarters," says Joe. "So forty
quarters makes how many dollars?"

"I don't know," says Kyle. He plays
with the quarters.

"You can do it, Kyle," says Joe. You're
a big boy, almost six years old!"

"I don't want to," says Kyle.

"Think," says Joe.

"Ten dollars!" says Mona. "Forty
quarters is ten dollars. There are ten dollars in a roll."

Joe looks at Mona. He wanted Kyle

to answer the question. Joe looks at Kyle. "Do you agree?"

"Yes," says Kyle. "Now can we start? I want to do quarters."

"Do you want to help, Joe?" asks Brita.

"I have to work," says Joe. But he does not really want to work. He wants to spend time with his family. Joe sits with Kyle. They separate all the quarters. Brita and Mona sit together on the other side. They take the other coins.

Joe watches while Kyle counts the quarters in groups of forty. He can do it when he wants to, but Joe worries: *Will Kyle be a good student?*

Joe also worries about Mona and Brita. He wants his sister-in-law to feel safe. He wants his wife to like Mona. Will it be difficult to have two mothers in one house?

Kyle interrupts his thoughts. He tries to put quarters in a paper roll, but the paper tears.

"This is stupid," says Kyle. "Why do they make it like this?"

"It's okay, Kyle," says Joe. "Try again."

Next time, Kyle is successful. He makes two rolls of quarters.

"Can I have these?" asks Kyle. "I want to buy a game."

"Not today," says Joe. "We need to buy food."

"But dad, there's a lot of money here!"

"Let's talk about something else.

What kind of game do you want?" asks Brita.

"A computer game," says Kyle.

"Maybe for your birthday," says Brita. "We'll use this money to buy oranges. You like oranges."

"Awww," says Kyle.

Brita puts the rolls of coins in a bag. "Maybe you can work in a bank someday. Then you can buy lots of computer games. Now come help me water the plants."

Mona watches them leave. "Joe, I want to get a job. I want to help pay the bills."

"We are fine. We don't have money problems."

"No, I don't believe you. You are counting quarters so you can buy food."

"That's not true. We are counting quarters so Kyle can learn math."

"And buy food."

"And because I get a lot of quarters at work."

"But I want to help."

"I know you do, Mona."

Mona gets up and looks out the window. There is a big yard with trees and plants. People are walking along the sidewalk with their dogs. Brita and Kyle are busy with the plants. *They do not know how lucky they are*, she thinks.

3. The Bank

Vincent parks outside the bank on Nineteenth Street. There are shops and a shipping store on one side. There is a hospital across the street. Trees shade the sidewalk and make a home for birds. Vincent gets out of the car and goes inside. His coworker Sylvia is already there.

"You look nice this morning, Vincent," says Sylvia. Then she smiles. "I have a strange feeling. Your true love will walk in that door today."

"I'm not getting my hopes up!" says Vincent.

"Maybe it's Adriana Bettencourt."

"Adriana Bettencourt? Who is she?"

"You see her every day!" says Sylvia. "The woman with the dress shop."

"Green shoes?"

"Yes, she always goes to your window. How about her?"

"I don't think so."

"How about the cook at the new restaurant?"

"Shini's Café? Shini's too young for me."

"She's not too young."

"She's only about thirty years old," says Vincent. "Anyway, she has a girlfriend."

"Maybe she has a sister," says Sylvia.

"Still too young," says Vincent.

"Are you really that old?" asks Sylvia.

"How old do you think I am?"

"Okay, thirty," says Sylvia.

"Guess again," says Vincent.

"Thirty-five?"

"Older," says Vincent.

"Forty?" Sylvia's eyes get bigger.

"Close. I'm forty-four."

"And you still live with your parents?"

"Why not? We get along," says Vincent.

"And does your mother cook for you?" Sylvia asks. "Wash your clothes?"

"What's wrong with that?" says Vincent. "She likes it."

"I bet you do, too," Sylvia says. "It keeps you young. I'm fifty-six with a family of my own, and I look eighty-five."

"You don't look eighty-five," Vincent smiles. "You look eighty-four."

Sylvia laughs.

A car drives up to Sylvia's window. Sylvia helps the customer. Vincent also has customers. An old man with a long white beard comes in. Behind him, Vincent sees Adriana Bettencourt.

Adriana hurries past the old man so she is first in line at Vincent's window.

"How are you Ms. Bettencourt?" asks Vincent.

"Call me Adriana," she says. "I'm well, thank you." Adriana gives Vincent some checks.

Vincent takes the checks. He looks at her deposit slip. The numbers are there, but the math is wrong. "You need to change these numbers," he says.

Adriana frowns. "I hate math!" She corrects the numbers on the deposit slip.

Vincent tries to be friendly, "How is business?"

"Terrible," she says. "This is a bad

year for weddings. I need a wedding. Did I tell you I have a dress shop?"

Vincent nods politely.

"I love helping a woman find the perfect dress, but the math part of business is boring."

"You could get a bookkeeper."

Adriana does not hear. "Too many women just wear yoga clothes. I don't get it."

"Maybe you can't do yoga in a dress," says Vincent.

Adriana frowns again. "There's more to life than yoga."

Vincent watches Adriana walk away. Sylvia notices and smiles.

The door opens again. Vincent sees Brita. Brita is another regular customer.

Brita's son, Kyle, is with her, and there is a new person. Vincent does not know the woman. A blue scarf covers her hair, and she is wearing a black dress. Vincent does not notice her clothes, though. He is looking at her eyes. She has large dark eyes, and there is a sadness in them. Vincent's heart jumps.

4. Bread

Rashid stays after class, and he almost misses the bus. When he gets on, he is out of breath. He sits across from a woman with green hair and a girl with a pink backpack. Rashid smiles, but they do not smile back. Rashid looks at his books. Then he looks out the window.

The bus stops, and the two women get off. Rashid sees the pink backpack. Quickly, he takes it and jumps off the bus. "Wait for me!" he tells the bus driver.

"Hey," Rashid calls out, but the woman with green hair walks faster. The little girl turns to look, but the older one pulls the little girl's hand.

"Your backpack!" Rashid yells louder. This time, the woman stops and turns. She is embarrassed when she sees the backpack.

"Sorry," she says.

Rashid smiles. "No problem." He looks up and sees the bus go down the street.

"You missed your bus," says the woman.

"It's okay," says Rashid. "I'm almost there. I'll walk."

"Well, thank you," she says. "My name is Sadie."

"I'm Rashid."

They walk and talk. Sadie works at a hospital on Nineteenth Street. Rashid knows the hospital. It is near his job at Shini's Café. Sadie knows Shini's. "Good soup," she says. They say goodbye, and Rashid walks a few blocks to work.

Shini is alone in the kitchen when Rashid arrives. She has short black hair. Her blue eyes look hard at Rashid, but she does not speak. Rashid puts away his backpack, washes his hands, and puts on a clean white apron.

The kitchen smells like chicken. Rashid can also smell vegetables. Shini is putting carrots into a pot.

"What are you making?" Rashid asks.

"Soup," she says. "Do you want to help?"

"Sure!"

"Today, the special is cream of carrot soup." Shini points to a pot with chicken, onions, and other vegetables.

"Never make soup with just water. In my restaurant, we don't waste anything. All the extra meat and vegetables add flavor." Shini takes the vegetables out of the pot. She adds cooked carrots and cream. Then she blends it into a beautiful orange soup.

"Is that it?" says Rashid. He looks at the creamy, orange soup.

"Taste it."

"Yum," says Rashid.

"Does it need anything else?" Shini asks, but it is not a real question. The soup is perfect.

"It's delicious," says Rashid. "Can I have some more?"

"No," she says. "We might be busy."

"It's so good," says Rashid.

"Just a little more." Shini gives

Rashid more soup. Then she gives him some bread. "I don't know why I'm doing this."

Rashid eats with his eyes closed. "So good!" he says.

"You like food, don't you?"

"Yes, I do," he says.

"Maybe you can work in the kitchen," Shini says. "Most cooks start like you. They wash dishes. Then they start cooking. I can teach you."

Rashid nods, "I'd like that."

"Can you cut onions?" asks Shini.

"Sure," Rashid says. "I do it for my mom all the time." He holds an onion in his hand and begins to cut.

"No, no, no, no, no!" Shini takes his knife away. "You'll hurt yourself."

"This way." She puts the onion on a

cutting board. Then she shows Rashid how to hold the onion safely. She picks up the knife and quickly chops the onion with her other hand.

Rashid's eyes are watering, but he watches. Shini gives him the knife.

"Now, you try it." She watches Rashid cut the onion. He feels slow and nervous.

"Don't stop. Keep going," Shini says. Then she gives Rashid a bag of onions.

"You just need practice," she says and goes back to the soup.

"Ouch!" says Rashid.

Shini comes over. Rashid has cut himself. There is blood on the knife and the cutting board.

"You just wasted an onion," Shini says. "Now clean this cut and cover it. When you come back, finish those onions."

"But it hurts," says Rashid.

"Do you want to cook or not?" asks Shini.

"I want to cook."

"Then keep working."

Rashid follows Shini's orders. Then he picks up the knife again. He chops onions for a long time. When he is finished, his eyes are red and watery, but the onions are done.

"Good," says Shini.

The waiters arrive, and then the customers. Rashid washes dishes, cleans tables, and makes salads. Time goes by quickly, and finally the waiters count out their money. They give a few dollars to Rashid and then leave together.

Rashid stays to wash the last dishes and clean the floor.

"Can I take this home?" He points to some extra bread.

Shini looks up from her computer.

"No, Rashid. We'll use the bread to make a dessert. Remember, we don't waste food here."

"Oh," says Rashid, "Sorry."

Shini sees his face. "Oh, take some," she says. "But just this one time."

Rashid puts the bread in a bag. "We never waste bread in my country either," he says. "It's wrong to waste bread."

Shini puts on her jacket. She holds the door open for Rashid, "You did well tonight, Rashid," she says.

The bus is late, so Rashid walks home. He likes working in the busy restaurant kitchen. He likes the excitement and the beautiful food.

Suddenly, Rashid falls over something. Then he hears someone call out. He sees two feet on the sidewalk. A man is sleeping in front of a store.

"Are you okay?" Rashid asks.

The man speaks, but Rashid cannot understand him.

Rashid takes out the bread. He puts it down next to the man. The man picks up the bread. He takes a bite, then another.

Rashid keeps walking. He worries about the man. It is hard to sleep on the street, but at least the man has food.

5. *The Cat*

The next day, Vincent arrives at the bank early. When Sylvia arrives, he is cleaning the windows.

"You look different today," Sylvia says. "What is it?"

"Nothing," says Vincent. "Why?"

"You're cleaning."

Vincent shrugs. Then he opens the doors. As usual, Adriana Bettencourt is waiting. She hurries to Vincent.

"How are you today?" he asks.

"Don't ask," she says. "You don't want to know."

"Okay," says Vincent. He takes her deposit slip and some checks.

"My cat is missing," says Adriana.

"Oh, I'm so sorry."

"She got out of the shop yesterday."

"Are you worried?"

"Yes, I'm very worried. She's a white cat with black feet. You might see her around here."

"Cats don't come into the bank very often," says Vincent.

Adriana does not laugh at Vincent's joke.

"Well, if you see her, call me! Here's my number." Adriana gives Vincent a piece of paper.

"I'm going to look for her now," says Adriana.

"I hope you find her," says Vincent.

"Thank you," says Adriana.

Sylvia watches her leave. "She likes you."

"No, she doesn't. She's always un-happy."

"She's not unhappy," Sylvia says. "She's nervous. You should invite her to dinner."

"I don't think so."

"It's none of my business, Vincent, but you need some romance in your life."

Suddenly the door opens. Vincent looks up and sees the woman with the beautiful eyes. She is with Joe this time. Vincent does not know what to do. He picks up some paper. He puts it down.

They go to Sylvia's window. The man gives Sylvia a withdrawal slip. He asks for $300.

"Why don't you use the ATM?" says

the woman. Vincent hears her voice. She must be from the same country as Joe. He tries to remember the country.

"I don't like ATMs," says Joe. "I like real people."

Sylvia smiles and counts the money. "Thank you, Joe," she says.

Joe gives the cash to the woman. "Here is $300."

"I don't want it." The woman shakes her head.

"Just take it, Mona. You need some spending money."

Now Vincent knows her name: Mona. He watches her walk to the door. She is smaller than Joe. Her back is straight, and she walks with confidence.

Mona feels his eyes. She turns and

looks at him. He looks away quickly. Then Mona and Joe leave. The door closes, and the bank is empty again.

Vincent looks out the window. Mona and Joe walk across the street. They turn onto Summer Street.

"Do they live on Summer Street?" asks Vincent.

"How should I know?" says Sylvia.

"Oh," Vincent says, "Sorry, I was just talking to myself."

Sylvia shrugs.

The piece of paper with Adriana Bettencourt's number falls on the floor. Vincent picks it up and looks at it. He has an idea.

At four o'clock, Vincent leaves by the front door. The sky is blue with a few white clouds. People are walking their dogs. Two people ride by on bicycles. Vincent passes his car and crosses Nineteenth Street. Then he goes up Summer Street. There are many small older houses with big yards. Children play outside.

Vincent is walking past a yellow house when he sees her. Mona is cutting flowers. She stands up suddenly and looks at Vincent.

"Hello," says Vincent.

"Hi," says Mona. She pushes her dark hair behind her scarf.

"I'm sorry to bother you," Vincent says, "but I'm looking for a lost cat. It's black with white feet."

Mona shakes her head. "What's your cat's name?"

Vincent cannot remember. "It's not

my cat. It, um, belongs to a friend."

"You don't know its name?"

"No," Vincent feels embarrassed, but he wants to keep the conversation going.

"Do you like cats?" he asks.

"Not really," she says, "but I don't tell people that."

Vincent nods, "I don't really like cats either."

Mona says, "It's nice you want to help your friend. I wouldn't pick up a strange cat."

"Well, she's not my friend, not really."

Mona looks at him with a question in her eyes. "The cat?"

"No, the woman," Vincent laughs nervously. "She's my customer."

Mona looks at Vincent closely, "Where do you work?"

"The bank on Nineteenth Street," he says.

"Oh, I was there today," Mona says.

"Were you?" asks Vincent.

"Yes," Mona is looking Vincent in the eyes. "I think I saw you."

Vincent tries to meet her eyes, but he looks down. "Anyway, it's a nice day. I thought I could help a customer and go for a walk at the same time."

Mona nods. "Well, I haven't seen it. But good luck!"

The door opens behind Mona, and Joe comes out. "Hi, Vincent. Is everything okay?" Joe asks.

"He's looking for a cat," Mona explains.

"That's right," says Vincent. He wants to stay and talk, but he does not have the right words, so he says goodbye.

Vincent walks down the street and stops. He is going the wrong way. Mona and Joe are still outside, though, so Vincent keeps going. It will take longer to get back to his car, but he feels shy.

Vincent is near the hospital when he sees a white cat with black feet. Vincent walks over to the cat. The cat smells his hand. He tries to pick up the cat, and it bites him. Vincent lets go of the cat. It runs away. Then he hears Adriana.

"Get her!" she says.

Vincent moves quickly. He picks up the cat again. The cat is angry, but now Adriana is there. She takes the cat.

Adriana looks at him, "You found her! Thank you!"

"It was nothing," says Vincent. He

looks at his hand. There is a little blood from the bite.

"Oh no! She bit you." Adriana speaks to her cat now. "That was not very nice, Percy." The cat does not care. It is trying to get down.

"I am so grateful," Adriana smiles at Vincent. "Let me take you to dinner."

Vincent is surprised. He does not know how to say "no." "That would be nice," he says politely.

Rashid walks to the store and buys carrots, onions, cream, and bread. When he comes out of the store, he looks at the sky. The white clouds are now darker. Wind is blowing the trees.

Rashid walks quickly, and he is home before the rain starts. He goes to the kitchen and starts to work. He sings while he chops onions and puts them in a pot. Then he starts on the carrots.

When Joe comes home, the kitchen smells delicious, but it looks terrible. There are dirty pots and food on the floor.

Rashid looks up from the soup with a big smile. "I'm making dinner." He looks very happy, and Joe does not want to hurt his feelings.

"Great!" Joe says. "I'll help."

"Oh, you don't need to," says Rashid. "I've got it."

"Well, let me wash some dishes. Brita will be home soon."

"I can do it."

"Let me help, Rashid." Joe changes his clothes quickly. He is cleaning the floor when Brita and Mona come in. They are laughing and wet from the rain.

"This is great!" Brita says to Mona, "The men are cooking!"

Mona laughs, "I'm hungry."

"You are going to love it, Mama," says Rashid. "This is a special night."

Everyone sits at the table, and Rashid serves dinner. The carrot soup is delicious. Kyle and his little brother Ethan want more, and Brita is surprised.

"You are a good cook," she says.

"Thank you," says Rashid.

"Can we get a dog?" asks Kyle.

"No, not now," says Joe.

"How about a cat?" Ethan asks. "I want a cat!"

Joe and Brita look at Mona.

"We'll talk about it later," says Brita. She changes the subject. "Rashid, why is tonight special?"

Everyone looks at Rashid. He takes a big breath and says, "I like cooking at Shini's."

Brita and Joe nod. Mona looks confused.

"And," says Rashid, "I've decided to open a restaurant."

"But how?" asks Mona. "You're going to be busy with medical school."

"Well, maybe medical school can wait," says Rashid.

"What?" Mona drops her spoon. It makes a loud noise on the plate.

Rashid looks at his mother, "I know I was thinking about becoming a doctor, but I changed my mind."

"You changed your mind?" Mona speaks more loudly. "You changed your mind?"

"Don't worry, Mama," Rashid says. "I've thought about it, and I've got a plan."

Everyone starts to speak, but Rashid holds up his hand. "Let me finish. Then you can talk. Medical school takes too long, and classes are too hard." Rashid looks at Joe. "It's more exciting to start a business like you did, Joe, and I can make money faster."

"That's crazy!" Mona starts to say, but Rashid interrupts her. "It's not crazy. Just listen. I can still go to college, but not right away. Working in a restaurant is better. I can get experience while I'm working. Shini will teach me."

"Rashid!" Mona tries to interrupt, but he continues. "I know you worry about money, Mama, so this is a better way."

"No, it's not," Mona says, but Rashid is louder. "I've thought about everything. First, I'll buy a food truck and sell food on the street. Customers will get to know me. Then I'll open the restaurant. I've thought about everything!"

"Cooking is a hard business," says Joe. "Most restaurants close after a short time."

"I know," says Rashid, "but I'm not like other restaurant owners. I can do it."

"Your father wanted you to be a doctor," says Mona.

Rashid takes a deep breath, "Please don't start, Mama."

"Your father was a doctor," Mona continues.

"I know," says Rashid.

Brita looks at Kyle and Ethan. Then she looks at Joe. "I'm going to take the boys upstairs."

"I'll check on you later," says Joe.

Mona begins to cry. "Your father died helping people. Don't you care?"

"Of course, I care," says Rashid.

"Food doesn't help people," says Mona.

"Is that what this is about? Helping people?" says Rashid. "Because I think *you* want a doctor in the family. That's your idea of success."

"What's wrong with that?" says Mona. "You can have a comfortable life in this country."

"A chef can have a comfortable life here, too," Rashid says.

"No," says Mona. "Not a cook!"

"I thought you might be happy for me," says Rashid more quietly. "But I see it now. You don't care about me. You only care about money."

"That's not true, Rashid, and you know it," Mona says. "You're young and you don't understand what you're saying."

"I think what Mona means, is …" Joe starts, but Rashid interrupts him. "Why is everyone against me?"

"We aren't against you," says Mona, "We just want the best for you!'""

"Do you even know what that is?" says Rashid. "Please stop planning my life. Plan your own life. You go to medical school!"

"You know I can't," says Mona.

Rashid stands up.

Mona keeps talking. "We are older,

and we know more. You need to sit down."

"No, I need to get out of here," Rashid leaves the room.

"Where are you going?" calls Mona.

The door opens and closes. Rashid is gone.

7. A Friend

Vincent and Adrianna are sitting inside a Mexican restaurant.

Adriana looks across the table at Vincent and smiles.

"Do you like Mexican food?"

"Of course! I love Mexican food," says Vincent.

"Good," Adriana says. "I don't usually like Mexican restaurants, but this one is okay."

Adriana drinks some water and looks at Vincent.

"Tell me about yourself. What do you do for fun?"

"I read."

"You read. What about?"

"History and adventure. I can travel in my mind."

"Oh?" Adriana asks. "An armchair traveler?"

"Yes. I like to learn about other countries."

"Are you bored with your life?"

"My life is good," says Vincent quickly. "I just don't have many adventures."

"Why don't you travel? You don't have children."

"My mother and father need me," says Vincent.

"Are they sick?"

"Kind of," says Vincent. "My mother has trouble breathing." He sees the waiter. "Do you think we can order?"

Adriana does not look at the waiter.

"I don't like to travel," she says. "Everywhere is the same."

"I'm not sure about that," says Vincent.

Finally, the waiter comes.

"I'll have the chicken soup," Vincent says. "I don't feel well."

"That's not adventurous," says Adriana. She orders enchiladas.

"Why do you sell dresses?" asks Vincent after the waiter leaves.

"An interesting question," Adriana takes a drink. "Do you know my shop?"

"It's near the bank. I walk by sometimes."

"Why don't you come in?"

"I don't need a dress."

Adriana laughs, "You're funny, Vincent. Why aren't you married?"

"I asked you a question first. The other day you said everyone wears yoga clothes, so why sell dresses? Why not sell yoga clothes?"

"I am glad you asked," Adriana says, "because I have an answer. Dresses are for special times in life. A woman buys a nice dress for a party or dinner with a nice man. Then when she looks at the dress later, she remembers. I like to be a part of that."

"Interesting," says Vincent. "But what if the party goes badly?"

"Then she gets rid of it and buys a new dress!"

The waiter puts their food on the table. Vincent eats his soup while Adriana talks about dresses. When the dinner is finally over, they put on their jackets and go outside. It is raining hard now, but they talk for a few minutes.

"I had fun tonight," Adriana says. "We should do this again some time."

"Yes," he says politely.

The rain is coming down harder, and Vincent drives slowly. Adriana is a smart, successful woman. Vincent likes her, but when he gets home, he is thinking about Mona. He turns off the car and puts his head in his hands.

8. A Search

Mona is worried about Rashid. She goes to the window and looks outside. The sky is black. Wind blows the rain onto the window. There is a flash of light and a loud boom. Mona jumps. Then she puts on her shoes and coat and hurries out the door.

Mona walks to Nineteenth Street. She passes the bank and shops. She walks to Shini's restaurant and looks in the window. Two customers are sharing a piece of cake. A waiter is sitting at the bar.

Mona opens the door. The waiter looks at her, "Table for one?" he asks.

"I'm Rashid's mother," Mona says.

"Rashid?"

"This is Shini's Café, isn't it? My son, Rashid, works here."

"Oh, he's not here," the waiter says.

"Are you sure? Do you know where he might be?"

The waiter shakes his head.

Mona turns to leave, but just then the chef comes out. She dries her hands on her apron and smiles at Mona. "Can I help you?"

"I'm looking for my son, Rashid. Did he come here?"

"No," Shini looks carefully at Mona. She sees a wet and worried mother. "He's not working tonight. He said he was going to make soup for his family."

"It was good," Mona says, "but we had an argument, and he left."

"I'm so sorry. I'm sure he'll come

back. The weather is terrible tonight." Shini turns to the kitchen.

"Wait," says Mona, "Do you have a minute?"

Shini looks around. The room is quiet, so she takes Mona to a small table and orders coffee from the waiter.

"How can I help you?" she asks.

"Rashid says he wants to be a cook, and I am hoping you can change his mind."

"Well, it's not really my business," Shini says.

"Can I tell you a story?"

Shini nods, and Mona continues, "You know we are from Syria. And you know there is a war, right?"

The waiter sets down two cups of coffee. Mona waits until he leaves. Then she continues. "My husband, Rashid's father, was a doctor. We lived in Syria. We had a good life in a beautiful neighborhood in Aleppo. Rashid was born, and he was such a happy child. Then the war started, and everything changed. Caleb didn't want to leave. He wanted to stay and help people. He didn't think they would bomb the hospital, but he was wrong. I was alone with Rashid when the bomb fell. It shook our house. Later, we learned the hospital had been bombed."

"I'm sorry," says Shini.

"Twenty-one doctors, thirty-three nurses, and 143 patients died. Sixteen were babies," Mona says.

"And your husband was killed."

"Yes. That was six years ago."

Shini nods. "And you want Rashid to be a doctor. It's a way to remember his father."

"Yes, his father wanted it. And Rashid wants it, too. I know he does, but he gets excited about new things, and he changes his mind. Right now, he just wants to chop vegetables!"

"There's nothing wrong with chopping vegetables," says Shini.

"I'm sorry. I didn't mean that. It's just … I know my son. He'll get bored with cooking, too."

"Look," says Shini. "This is going to sound strange, but I need to tell you something."

"What?"

"I am a doctor."

"I don't understand," says Mona. "You're a cook!"

"I'm a doctor. I went to medical school," says Shini.

"What?" Mona is surprised.

"Medical school was my parents' plan for me. I didn't want to disappoint them, so I studied medicine."

"What happened?" Mona is quiet now.

"I was a doctor for five years," Shini says, "but I hated it."

"No job is perfect," Mona says. "Sometimes you have to do things you don't like."

"I don't agree. A person spends a lot of days in a job. The hospital was too white, too clean, and there were too many rules. I was very unhappy, and one day I asked myself, 'Do you really want to do this for the rest of your life?' The answer was 'no.' I love colors, people, food, and the craziness of a restaurant kitchen. I quit and opened this place."

"Oh, your poor parents!" says Mona.

"That's not how I see it," says Shini. "Doctors are important. It's not wrong to be a doctor. Your husband was a brave and good man, but Rashid has to follow his heart."

Mona stares at her coffee. She is thinking about Shini's words. Suddenly, she feels cold. "I have to go," she pushes away her coffee and gets up. "Something's wrong. I can feel it."

Light shines from an upstairs window of the yellow house. Brita and Kyle are reading in Kyle's bed. When the story is over, Kyle says, "Can we get a dog?"

Brita sets the book on a table. "When we get a dog, what do you want to name it?"

"Lucky," says Kyle. "Because it'll be a lucky dog."

"And you'll be a lucky boy," says Brita.

Then she hears Ethan come in. It is raining hard, and he cannot sleep either. Ethan climbs up and sits on Brita's other side.

"Want cat," says Ethan.

"What will you name your cat?" Brita asks.

"Happy," says Ethan.

"Happy and Lucky! What great names!" Brita says.

They talk until the boys fall asleep. Then Brita hears Joe come up the stairs.

"Hey," he says quietly.

"Hey, there," Brita says. "The boys want a pet."

Joe looks sad, "We can't right now."

"Yes, I know." Brita tries to sit up without waking the boys. "Do you want to help me get this one in bed?"

Joe picks up the sleeping Ethan and puts him in his bed. Then they make tea.

"So Rashid didn't come home, and Mona is out looking for him," Joe says.

"I know," says Brita. "Is she okay out there?"

"I keep telling myself that the biggest danger in this neighborhood is the cats."

Brita laughs, "Mona doesn't like cats."

"I know," Joe says. "She has strong feelings about them."

"Yes, she does!" Brita agrees. "She feels strongly about a lot of things."

"Including Rashid. I should help her look for him."

"I knew you were going to say that," Brita says. "Go, but be careful."

Joe puts on his jacket.

"Don't forget your phone!" Brita says, but it is too late. He is gone.

Brita is washing the dishes when she sees a light. It is Joe's phone. The screen has the name of a hospital. Brita's heart jumps. She answers Joe's phone. A woman asks if she knows Rashid.

"I'm his relative. What happened?"

"There was a car accident," says the woman. "He's here in the hospital."

"Is he alive?"

"Yes."

"What can you tell me?"

"Just that the doctors are with him now."

When Brita hangs up, she calls her neighbor Dolores. Dolores gets out of bed and comes to stay with the boys. Brita grabs her jacket and goes out in the rain to look for Joe. She finds him on Winter Street. When he hears Brita's news, his face turns white. She hands him the phone, "You're going to have to tell Mona."

Joe makes the call. He is speaking Arabic now. Brita does not understand the words, but she very much understands Mona's cry of pain.

Rashid opens his eyes. He sees a woman with green hair. He knows her, but he does not know how.

"Where am I?" he says.

"Shhh," says the nurse. "You had an accident. Don't try to move."

Rashid's head hurts. He wants to sit up, but he cannot.

"Do you remember me?" asks the nurse. "You brought us my sister's backpack."

"I did?" asks Rashid. Then he remembers, "Sadie?"

"Yes," says the nurse. "Small world, isn't it? Now rest. We're going to take care of you."

There is a noise outside Rashid's

room. The doctors are calling. They are taking someone to a different room. Rashid closes his eyes. He sleeps some more.

Suddenly, Rashid wakes up. He hears his mother's voice. The door opens, and Mona runs to the bed and hugs him.

"Ouch," says Rashid. "Mama, you're hurting me! Not that hand!"

Mona takes Rashid's other hand. "Why did you do that?" she asks. "Why did you jump in front of that car?"

"I didn't."

"The driver said you did. It was raining, and you ran right in front of him. You went over the top of his car, Rashid."

"Are you sure it wasn't a truck?"

"Don't joke! You almost died!"

Rashid tries to sit up, but he is in

pain. He looks at his mother. "I don't remember."

Joe appears behind Mona. "Your mother is right. You ran in front of a car. The driver tried to stop. He hit you and you went over the top of the car. You injured your head and your arm."

"Am I going to be okay?"

"Yes," says Sadie. "But you need to rest."

Rashid looks at his mother. "It's not your fault," he says.

"Of course, it's not my fault," she says. "You always do this. You run in the street, and you don't look."

"It was dark," says Rashid.

Mona shakes her head, "I thought you would be safe here with Joe and

Brita. But it doesn't matter where you go. You always get in trouble."

"I know I disappoint you," says Rashid. "I can't be the son you want, Mama. I'm not perfect like my father."

"Don't say that," says Mona.

Joe shakes his head. "Actually, you *are* like your father."

"I doubt it," says Rashid.

"You didn't know him when he was twenty. Your father was adventurous, too," says Joe.

"But that's not important," says Mona. "The point is, he worked hard, and he gave his family a good life."

"I'm just saying that Rashid is young, and we sometimes forget what that's like."

Rashid nods. "Uncle Joe's right. Sometimes I think you don't really know me, Mama. Maybe I'm not smart enough for medical school. Maybe opening a restaurant is the best thing for me."

Mona starts to speak, but the door opens again. It is Shini.

"Here you are!" Shini says. "The nurse sent me to the wrong room. I almost gave your soup to an old woman in Room 305." Shini puts a bag on the table. "I worried you might have to eat hospital food."

Mona introduces Shini to Joe.

"It's nice to meet you," says Joe. "We were just talking about Rashid's plans. He wants to open a restaurant like yours. That can't be easy!"

Shini agrees. "No, it's not easy." She

turns to Rashid, "Opening a restaurant is not easier than becoming a doctor. Believe me, I know because I did both. The important thing is that you do it for the right reasons."

"What are the right reasons?" Rashid asks

"You have to be excited about your work," says Shini. "You are going to spend a lot of hours doing it!"

"But—" says Mona.

"Look, I really just wanted to drop off this soup. My girlfriend is waiting," says Shini. "I hope you feel better soon, Rashid." She leaves.

Rashid waits until she leaves, "She's right. My job has to mean something to me."

"What is more meaningful than

medicine?" asks Mona. "It's my job as your mother to help you make a good decision. What if you waste your life?"

"Maybe it's time to stop asking that question. Maybe you need a different question," says Rashid.

"What's that?" Mona asks.

"What about you? What if you waste your life?"

11. Sweet Tea

Vincent helps his mother and father to the waiting area in the hospital. He is reading the news on his phone when he hears voices. Vincent looks up. Joe, Brita, and the two boys come into the waiting area. Then he sees Mona.

"He's going to be okay. That's the most important thing," says Joe.

The family sits across from Vincent and his parents. The older boy sits with Brita, and the younger one sits with Joe. Mona sits next to Brita. Brita holds Mona's hand.

Vincent looks down. He is near Mona again, but why is she here? He wants to talk to her, but how? He stands up.

"Do you need anything?" Vincent asks his mother. She shakes her head, but his father asks for sweet tea. Vincent goes to the machines. He is putting quarters in when he hears someone. Vincent turns around. Mona is standing there. When she sees him, she steps back.

"I'm sorry," Mona says. "I didn't mean to surprise you. I was thinking about something else."

"Oh, it's no problem," says Vincent. I'm a little nervous myself." He takes the tea from the machine and starts to walk away. Then he says, "Do you remember me? We talked on the street. I was looking for a cat."

"A cat?" Mona looks confused.

Vincent continues. "You were cutting

flowers, and I walked by. Maybe you don't remember. It was a few days ago."

"Oh, right," Mona says. "Your friend's cat. Did you find it?"

"Yes. She is not my friend exactly. Hey, are you okay?"

"Yes, fine. I mean, I'm fine."

"That's good," says Vincent, "because you are here, in a hospital."

"My son got hit by a car," Mona says. "He's hurt. But the doctors say he will recover."

"Oh, I'm sorry to hear that," Vincent moves out of the way so Mona can put money in the machine. She puts four quarters in and tries to buy water. The machine does not work.

"You need eight quarters," says Vincent.

Mona only has seven. Vincent has an extra quarter, and he gives it to her. His hand touches her hand.

"Thank you," says Mona. She chooses sweet tea, and they stand for a moment. Vincent wants to keep talking, but he is nervous.

"I like hot tea," she says. "But this is okay."

"Me too," says Vincent. It is not true. Vincent likes cold sweet tea, but he wants to agree with her.

"Are you okay?" asks Mona. "You are in a hospital, too."

"Oh, I'm fine." Vincent tells Mona about his mother. "She is here often," Vincent says. "She has asthma."

Mona nods and tells Vincent about her husband. "He was a doctor. He helped people with breathing problems." Then she tells him about the war.

"I'm sorry," says Vincent. "And now you live here with your husband's relatives?"

Mona tells Vincent about Brita and Joe. "They're very nice to me. I feel grateful, but I'm a lot of trouble."

"Maybe not. Maybe you make their life more interesting," says Vincent.

Mona is surprised. "I'm not sure they want a more interesting life."

"I don't know. It's nice to help when someone needs you," says Vincent.

"I agree!" says Mona, "But I want to be the helper. It's hard to be the person in trouble."

"I understand," says Vincent. "I am the same way."

"Right now, I want to help my son, but everyone is telling me to leave him alone."

"What do you mean?" Vincent asks.

"I don't know why I'm telling you this."

"It's okay. Sometimes it's good to talk to someone outside the family," says Vincent.

"Well, he needs to make some decisions about college. He is supposed to go to medical school, but he changes his mind every day." Mona tells Vincent about her argument with Rashid. "Then he ran out the door, and that's how he got hit by a car."

"It's not your fault," says Vincent.

"I know, but it tells you about Rashid. He has strong feelings."

"Maybe he's like his mother," says Vincent. He knows his parents and Mona's family are watching them, but he does not care. Mona is talking to him. Her eyes are red, and she looks sleepy, but she is beautiful.

When the doctors call his mother's name, he does not want to leave Mona, but he must go with his family, and she must go to hers.

12. A Job

A few days later, a doctor and two medical students visit Rashid's room. Mona stands up. She is waiting for news, and it is good. When the doctor says Rashid can go home, she cries.

"Why are you crying, Mama?" asks Rashid.

"I can't help it," says Mona. "I am so grateful!"

Sadie comes in with a bowl of soup. "It's from Shini," she says. "I broke the rules and warmed it up in the break room."

"You should try it," Rashid says. "Shini makes the best soup in Houston."

"I know!" says Sadie. She turns to

Mona. "It's good to see him eating, isn't it?"

"I worry about him so much," says Mona.

"I know, but he'll be fine," Sadie says. "Don't worry."

"I have to worry," says Mona. "I'm his mother."

"But it isn't a job," Sadie says. Her words surprise Mona.

"You are the second person to tell me that." Mona looks at Rashid and back at Sadie. "I just don't understand Rashid. When I was a girl, I wanted to be a doctor, but my parents didn't have much money. They could only send one child to college."

"Who did they send?" asks Sadie.

"My older brother."

"Is he a doctor?"

"Yes, of course. And now Rashid can be a doctor, but he doesn't want to," Mona says.

"I can hear you," Rashid says. His eyes are closed. He is sleepy but not asleep.

Sadie notices. She picks up the empty soup bowl and leads Mona to the waiting area. "You never know," she says in a quiet voice. "He might change his mind three more times."

"I know Rashid wants to decide for himself, but what if he makes a bad decision?" Mona says.

"Then he makes a bad decision," says Sadie.

For the second time Mona looks at

Sadie in surprise. She does not have an answer.

They are quiet for a moment. Then a woman in a yellow dress and green shoes comes in.

Sadie looks up. "Hello, Adriana!" The woman comes over, and Sadie introduces her. "Adriana sells the most beautiful dresses," she tells Mona. Then she turns to Adriana. "Mona is the mother of my friend, Rashid. He got hit by a car."

"Oh, I'm sorry to hear that," says Adriana. "Drivers are terrible these days. How is he?"

"He's going to make it," says Mona.

"Good," says Adriana. "Young people are strong."

"I hope you aren't sick," says Sadie to Adriana.

"No, not at all. But I've got an appointment with Doctor Crocker." She smiles. "For dinner."

"Oh, good for you," Sadie smiles. "Dr. Crocker needs to have some fun. He works too hard."

"I'll try to change that," says Adriana. "I ran into him when I took my cat for a checkup. We started talking. It turns out we're both cat people!"

Sadie nods. "I've got to get back to work." She turns to Mona. "Don't worry about Rashid. He's a good person. He's going to find his way."

Sadie walks through the doors and back to the nurse's station.

"I hope you don't mind my asking, but what was that about?" Adriana sits across from Mona.

"My son doesn't want to go to medical school."

"Oh, too bad," says Adriana. "It's nice to have a doctor in the family. What does he want to do?"

"Chop vegetables."

Adriana laughs. "Well, it's nice to have a good cook in the family, too."

Mona does not laugh. "He wants a food truck."

"Kids these days," says Adriana. "I don't have any myself. Too much trouble."

"He's more trouble than most," says Mona. "Maybe that's why I love him so much."

Adriana nods, "Well, I don't know about parenting, but I do know one thing. Running a business is hard."

Adriana tells Mona about her shop. "You have to be good at everything. I'm great at fashion and sales, but I'm terrible at math. It gives me a headache."

"I'm not so good at sales," says Mona, "but I love math."

"Can you do bookkeeping?"

"Yes, actually. I was an accountant in my country."

"Were you? I need a bookkeeper."

Mona looks thoughtful. "I can do that. It's easy."

"Are you working now?" Adriana looks at Mona. "Maybe I can give you a job."

"Thank you, but I have to take care of my son," says Mona.

"It's not too much, and you can work at home."

"Really?" says Mona. "I need to think about it. Can I let you know tomorrow?"

"Yes, of course," says Adriana. She gives Mona her number. "Call me and we can discuss the details." Suddenly she looks up.

"What is it?" Mona turns to look.

Adriana says quietly, "Can you help me?"

Mona nods.

"Will you talk to that man from the bank? His name is Vincent. I think he likes me, but I have plans with someone else. I don't want to hurt his feelings."

Mona laughs, "Oh, I see. Sure, I'll talk to Vincent."

"You know him?"

"A little," says Mona.

On the other side of the room,

Vincent is not sure what to do. He sees Mona, and he smiles. Then he sees Adriana, and he stops.

Adriana gets up. "Hi, Vincent," she looks at her watch. "Vincent, I think you know Mona. You two have a lot in common. She knows how to count money, too."

She turns to Mona and says in a quiet voice, "Call me." Then Adriana hurries to meet a man in a doctor's white coat. Mona watches them. Then she sighs and turns to Vincent.

Vincent walks over.

"How is your son?"

"He's fine, just fine," says Mona. "He's eating."

"That's wonderful news!" says Vincent.

"And guess what else? I've got a job!"

"Oh, are you happy about it?"

"Yes. Today is my lucky day," Mona says. "I'm going to get some sweet tea and celebrate. Would you like to come?"

"Yes," says Vincent. "It's my lucky day, too." He follows her out the door.

13. Change

Rashid returns to work on a Saturday night. The air is fresh and cool. People are out walking, and the café is busy.

"You look a little thin," Shini says.

"I'm fine," says Rashid.

"Your face is still green on one side."

"It was purple," says Rashid.

"I know," says Shini. "It'll turn yellow, and then it'll be gone."

"You're a doctor. You know," says Rashid.

"The body is an amazing thing. And you are young. Now, are you ready to work?"

"Yes!"

Rashid puts on a clean, white apron and goes to his station. He cuts vegetables and makes salads. There is a new dishwasher.

"Your family is here," says one of the waiters as he pushes open the kitchen door.

Rashid goes to the kitchen door and looks out. Joe is pointing to a table in the corner, Brita is carrying Ethan and holding Kyle's hand. Rashid looks for his mother, but she is not with them.

In the dining room, Brita puts Ethan on a high seat. Then she sits down across from Joe.

"We should call Mona," Joe says. "She's alone in that apartment over Adriana's shop. Maybe she wants to join us."

"I did," says Brita. "She said she's busy."

Joe is surprised. "Did she say why?"

Brita shakes her head. Then the waiter comes. They order pizza and salad. When he leaves, Joe frowns.

"Is she okay?"

"Of course! She has a job and an apartment, and she's making new friends."

"I worry about her," says Joe.

"She'll be fine. It's good to meet new people."

"Yes, but—"

"Don't forget. You and I were strangers once." Brita smiles at Kyle and Ethan, "Do you know how your father and I met? I was at a coffee shop, and I spilled my coffee. Your father helped me clean it up."

"And I went to that coffee shop every

day after that," Joe says. "I was hoping your mother would come back."

Kyle asks his mother, "Did you go back?"

"Yes. I had a feeling about him. I knew he was special."

A few minutes later, Rashid brings their pizza. "I thought I'd say 'hi,'" he says. "I put extra mushrooms on it."

"No!" says Kyle. "I hate mushrooms."

"Just kidding," says Rashid. "I know what you like."

"Extra cheese!"

"Then this must be yours!"

"Where is my mother?" Rashid asks Brita. "Didn't she come with you?"

"She had other plans."

Rashid frowns, "She didn't tell me."

"She's a grown woman!" says Brita. "She doesn't have to tell us everything."

"Yeah, but we're still family."

"Hey, I know where she is." Brita looks over Joe's shoulder. Rashid and Joe turn. A waiter is seating Mona and Vincent at an outdoor table.

"Oh, look at that," says Joe.

Rashid frowns. "Who is that man?"

"Vincent. He works at the bank. I think they met at the hospital."

"Why didn't anyone tell me?" says Rashid. "Should I go meet him?"

"Later," says Brita. "Give them some space."

Rashid sighs. He walks back to the kitchen. Then he turns and looks at his mother. He looks at Brita, then he shrugs and disappears through the door.

"He's also going to have to get used to a change." Brita puts a piece of pizza on everyone's plate. "Careful," she says. "It's hot."

Ethan tries to pick up a piece and drops it. Tomato sauce gets on his shirt, and he cries. Brita helps him clean it up.

Joe does not notice. He is watching Vincent and Mona through the window.

14. A New Life

Outside, at a table under a tree, Vincent tells Mona about a funny customer.

"Randy is about eighty years old, and he has a long white beard. He's polite, but every time he comes in, he asks for a pen. Then he forgets to give it back. He must have 100 bank pens."

Mona laughs. "Why does he need so many pens?"

"I have no idea, but he also eats our cookies. Every day he walks by and looks in the window. If there are cookies out, he comes in and gets one."

"Only one?"

"Actually, two, sometimes three."

"He's probably a very rich man."

Mona laughs again, and Vincent feels happy. "I like it when you laugh," he says.

Mona smiles, "I like to laugh."

"Well, hopefully you can laugh more now. Your son is out of the hospital, and you have a new job."

"I still worry about Rashid, but I'm going to give him some space. That's what you do here in the US, right? You give people space."

"We do," Vincent laughs.

"And we don't!" Mona laughs. "Family business is everyone's business."

The waiter brings some bread, and Mona breaks off a piece and puts butter on it. "I have to learn from you," she says. "I need to become more American."

"Are you happy you came here?"

"Oh yes, but Syrians have a different culture. It's hard to change."

"I don't know what that's like," says Vincent. "I've lived here all my life."

"Everything is new here: the buildings, stores, and cars. And people are so happy. I keep seeing these shirts. They have smiling people, and they say, 'Life is good.'"

"Life *is* good, isn't it?"

"Yes, but not always, not for Syrians."

"Of course."

"Even with the pain, I miss my country."

"What do you miss?"

"Aleppo is … was beautiful. There were roses everywhere, and when I walked to the market, I passed through history. There are … were a lot of famous old buildings in Aleppo." Mona looks away, remembering.

"I would like to see Aleppo," says Vincent. "It's one of the oldest cities in the world."

"How do you know about Aleppo?"

"I read a lot of books, but I've never met anyone from Syria."

"Until now," says Mona.

"I want to learn more. I think you're interesting."

"Be careful what you wish for!" Mona laughs.

"You can teach me."

"Okay, here's something: *Alhamdillilah*. Can you say it?"

"What does it mean?"

"Praise be to God. We say it when we are grateful, and when we have hope. It's not just for my religion, either. It's for everyone. We say it all the time!"

"*Alhamdillilah*?"

"Yes."

"So if I have good luck, I can say it?" says Vincent.

"Yes, to show your gratitude."

"Like, if I find a parking place?"

"Yes."

"Or if my mother gets out of the hospital?"

"Absolutely."

"And if a beautiful and interesting woman comes into my life?" Vincent looks at Mona.

She smiles and looks down. "Yes," she says.

"*Alhamdillilah*," says Vincent. "I am grateful."

"Life is good," says Mona.